THE CITY OF

INTERCONNECTION

Seven Cities of Mars — Book Six

B.K. Anderson

COPYRIGHT PAGE

This is a work of fiction. Names, characters, places, and incidents are either

Published by B.K. Anderson

ISBN: 9798995914822

Cover Design by B.K. Anderson

Printed in the United States of America

SERIES PAGE

The Seven Cities of Mars

1. The City of Enduring Light

2. The City of Silence

3. The City of Flowing Currents

4. The City of Restraint

5. The City of Passage

6. The City of Interconnection

7. The City of the Seventh Heart

DEDICATION

For those who discovered

that survival alone was never enough.

And for those who learned

that life continues

only when we belong to one another.

EPIGRAPH

"The hive was never many.

It was always one."

— The Listener

REFLECTION

There are worlds that survive through strength.

There are worlds that survive through knowledge.

And there are worlds that survive only when every living thing remembers it belongs to every other.

Mars had once forgotten this.

The ancient cities beneath the red sands had been built by races who mastered energy, movement, silence, restraint, and passage. Yet even the greatest

civilizations had failed when they began

to believe themselves separate.

One by one, the currents between them

weakened.

The woven field unraveled.

The great resonance faded into isolation.

But life does not surrender easily.

Deep beneath the recovering plains of

Mars, hidden systems still listened for

connection. The bees carried it. The bogs

remembered it. And somewhere within

the sleeping foundations of the sixth city,

an ancient network waited for enough

living hearts to choose one another again.

Asa did not yet understand what the bees

had been teaching him all along.

No living thing survives alone.

And some awakenings cannot begin until

many lives learn to move as

one.

Table of Contents

COPYRIGHT PAGE 2

SERIES PAGE 4

The Seven Cities of Mars 4

DEDICATION 5

EPIGRAPH 6

REFLECTION 7

Prelude 12

Chapter 1 — The Threads Beneath 14

Chapter 2 — Signals Without Meaning 21

Chapter 3 — The Silent Corridors 30

Chapter 4 — The Woven Field 40

Chapter 5 — Fracture Points 51

Chapter 6 — The Hive Lesson 63

Chapter 7 — Shared Breath 67

Chapter 8 — Resonance Paths 77

Chapter 9 — The Listener Between Minds 88

Chapter 10 — The Forgotten Threads 99

Chapter 11 — The Garden Above 113

Chapter 12 — The Child and the Hive 124

Chapter 13 — The Song of Many Voices 138

Chapter 14 — The City Awakens 152

Chapter 15 — The Fear of Dissolving 165

Chapter 16 — The Great Exchange 178

Chapter 17 — Asa's Realization 193

Chapter 18 — The Interwoven Heart 206

Chapter 19 — The Pulse Beyond Mars   220 Chapter 20 — The Stirring of the Seventh Heart.. 233

Chapter 21 — The First Invitation 244

Chapter 22 — The Quiet Returning 257

Chapter 23 — A City That Lives 269

Chapter 24 — The First Pathway Home................ 281

Prelude

The first signal was almost too small to notice.

A single bee changed direction in midair.

Not randomly.

Not from wind.

It turned as though it had heard something far below the surface of Mars.

Then another followed.

And another.

Until the entire hive shifted as one living

current beneath the dim amber sky.

Chapter 1 — The Threads Beneath

The first signal was almost too small to notice.

A single bee altered its course beneath the amber haze of the Martian sky, drifting away from the familiar gathering pattern the hive had followed since their arrival near the recovering plains. Asa might have dismissed the movement as random disturbance had the second and third not followed within moments. Soon the entire current of bees shifted together, not scattering in confusion but flowing with quiet purpose toward a distant rise of dark stone partially buried beneath the sands. Their hum deepened as they moved, carrying through the thin air with a resonance he felt more within his chest than through his ears. Beside him, Saxifraga stood motionless upon the ridge, her pale gaze fixed upon the distant structures emerging through layers of drifting dust.

The City of Interconnection did not rise from Mars in the same manner as the previous cities they had encountered.

Enduring Light had awakened slowly

beneath ancient stillness, while Silence

had hidden itself so completely that even

sound seemed reluctant to cross its

thresholds. Flowing Currents had stirred

through movement, and Passage had

revealed itself through corridors waiting

to be crossed. Yet this city appeared

wounded by division long before their

arrival. Portions of its outer structures

glowed faintly beneath the sand, only to

darken again moments later. Thin lines of

pale illumination traveled through

fractured towers like weakened nerves struggling to remember forgotten pathways. Entire sections awakened briefly, shimmered with life, and then collapsed once more into shadow.

Asa felt unease settle within him as the bees continued downward along the slope. The city did not seem dead. In many ways, that troubled him more. It behaved like a living thing trapped between waking and collapse, aware enough to struggle yet unable to fully rise. Far below, enormous bridgeways stretched between partially exposed towers, many broken in places where centuries of shifting sands had torn them apart. He noticed movement within distant openings, though whether drifting dust or functioning mechanisms he could not tell. The bees showed no hesitation. Their shared hum thickened steadily as they approached the fractured outer boundary, as though something beneath the ancient stone had already recognized them.

"The city listens," Saxifraga said softly.

Her voice carried no fear, yet Asa heard caution beneath the calmness. He turned toward her, watching the faint silver patterns moving slowly beneath the surface of her skin. He had learned enough through the awakening cities to recognize when she sensed old systems stirring around them. Mars itself seemed quieter here. Even the wind crossing the plains moved in uncertain currents, shifting direction without warning before fading into unnatural stillness. Ahead of them, another pulse of light moved beneath the exposed foundations. This time the illumination traveled farther through the buried structures before abruptly vanishing, as though the city had attempted to complete a thought and failed before reaching its end.

Behind them, the hive continued its descent toward the broken gates of the sleeping city.

Chapter 2 — Signals Without Meaning

The outer gates of the City of Interconnection had once been vast enough to admit entire processional caravans beneath their arching spans. Even buried beneath centuries of drifting dust, the remaining structures dwarfed the travelers approaching them now. Asa slowed beside the descending hive as the bees crossed through shadows cast by fractured towers leaning at uneasy angles against one another. Thin currents of pale light flickered intermittently beneath the stone beneath his feet, illuminating ancient pathways before vanishing again without pattern. Nothing within the city maintained consistency for long. Every awakening seemed followed by collapse, as though countless unseen systems struggled to remember how they were meant to function together.

What disturbed Asa most was the behavior of the bees themselves.

Individual workers moved with uncertainty unlike anything he had witnessed before. Small groups separated from the greater current without warning,

circling exposed walls or drifting into

darkened openings only to emerge

moments later and abruptly change

direction again. Several landed

motionless against ancient surfaces, their

antennae vibrating rapidly as though

attempting to interpret signals too faint or

fragmented to understand. Yet despite the

confusion of the individual movements,

the hive as a whole continued progressing

steadily inward. No collisions occurred.

No panic spread through the swarm. The

greater pattern remained intact even while

countless smaller motions appeared disordered and uncertain.

Saxifraga knelt beside a partially exposed section of black stone where narrow veins of light pulsed beneath translucent layers embedded within the ancient material. Her fingertips rested lightly upon the surface as she closed her eyes. Asa had seen her commune with the older systems before, though never with such hesitation. Usually the cities responded to her presence with recognizable rhythms, as though ancient mechanisms still acknowledged the lineage she carried within her blood. Here the responses came unevenly. The faint glow beneath her hand brightened suddenly, spreading through branching lines extending into the buried structures beyond, only to fracture moments later into scattered pulses traveling in conflicting directions.

"It cannot hold coherence," she said quietly.

Asa looked upward toward the distant towers where entire sections of the city shimmered briefly into illumination.

Through narrow openings high above, he glimpsed movement within suspended corridors connecting one structure to another. For an instant he believed figures crossed there in silence. Then darkness returned, swallowing the passageways completely. A low vibration moved through the stone beneath them shortly afterward, subtle enough to escape notice had the bees not reacted immediately. The scattered workers shifted direction all at once, abandoning whatever signals had drawn them moments before as the greater hive altered course toward a descending avenue partially buried beneath layers of sand.

The movement unsettled him because no command appeared to pass between them.

No single bee guided the others. No visible pattern explained how the hive maintained unity while its individual members behaved as though lost within conflicting currents. Asa followed slowly behind, watching one worker spiral uncertainly near his shoulder before abruptly accelerating toward the deeper passages below. It occurred to him then that the confusion belonged not to the bees themselves, but to the signals surrounding them. Something within the City of Interconnection continued transmitting across damaged pathways, sending fractured impulses through systems no longer capable of carrying them cleanly. The hive responded as living water might respond to broken channels—scattering briefly at each fracture before finding the greater flow once more.

Far beneath the dim horizon of Mars,

another pulse traveled through the

wounded city.

This time Asa felt it inside his own chest.

Chapter 3 — The Silent Corridors

The descending avenue carried them deeper beneath the fractured outer districts of the city, where the wind from the Martian plains no longer reached them. Sand still drifted through broken openings high above, though here it fell slowly in narrow streams that shimmered through scattered pulses of pale light. Asa became increasingly aware that the silence within the buried structures was unlike ordinary stillness. It pressed against the senses with unnatural weight, as though the city itself strained to hear sounds long absent from its corridors. Even the bees lowered their hum as they moved farther inward, their collective tone softening into a subdued resonance that seemed absorbed by the surrounding stone.

The passage broadened ahead into a vaulted chamber lined with towering arches woven from dark metallic material Asa could not fully identify. The surfaces appeared smooth at first glance, yet beneath the dim illumination he saw countless fine lines threading through the walls like frozen currents beneath black ice. At irregular intervals, faint pulses traveled along those hidden channels before disappearing into adjoining corridors branching deeper into the city. Some pathways remained entirely dark. Others awakened briefly with flickering light before failing once more. The city behaved less like machinery and more like a damaged nervous system attempting to reconnect scattered memories of itself.

Several bees drifted ahead into one of the side corridors.

Almost immediately, Asa heard something.

Not words.

Not even distinct sound.

It resembled the faint echo of distant movement carried through impossible depth, as though countless footsteps once traveled those passageways long ago and the city still remembered their passing.

He stopped beside one of the arches,

listening carefully. For a brief moment he thought he heard voices layered far beneath the silence. The tones remained too faint to distinguish, rising and falling like fragments of forgotten conversations buried within the stone itself. Then the corridor darkened completely, and the echoes vanished as abruptly as they had appeared.

Saxifraga remained motionless near the center of the chamber. Her silver gaze followed the dim pulses moving through the walls while the pale markings beneath her skin brightened faintly in response.

Asa had learned to trust those subtle

changes. The cities recognized her

presence even when their systems no

longer fully functioned. Yet here he

sensed uncertainty within the ancient

responses surrounding them. The

corridors awakened only in fragments, as

though different portions of the city

attempted communication without

awareness of one another. A nearby arch

illuminated suddenly from base to

ceiling, revealing intricate symbols

flowing across its inner surface before the

light fractured into scattered
interruptions.

"It is trying to speak," Saxifraga said
quietly.

The words sent a chill through Asa
despite the still air surrounding them. He
turned slowly, studying the endless
corridors extending into darkness beyond
the chamber. For the first time since
entering the city, he no longer felt they
were simply exploring abandoned
structures. Something beneath the
fractured systems remained aware of their

presence. Not fully awake. Not fully coherent. Yet listening.

Then another vibration passed through the chamber.

This one stronger.

Lights surged simultaneously through multiple corridors, spreading outward in widening patterns that illuminated distant passageways disappearing far beneath the city. The bees reacted instantly. Their subdued hum deepened into a unified resonance that filled the vaulted chamber like a living current. One by one, darkened corridors began pulsing in response. Somewhere within the depths beyond their sight, enormous systems stirred briefly toward life before fading once more into uncertain silence.

And from far below, carried upward through the buried arteries of the city, came the unmistakable echo of movement approaching them through the dark.

Asa paused beside the fractured corridor as movement crossed the distant intersection ahead. For a moment he believed he had seen a child standing beneath the failing lights. Yet when he stepped forward, only drifting dust and the fading pulse of the walls remained.

Chapter 4 — The Woven Field

The deeper chambers of the City of Interconnection did not reveal themselves all at once. Pathways unfolded gradually as scattered systems awakened in fragments around the travelers, offering brief glimpses into structures hidden beneath centuries of silence before darkness reclaimed them again. Asa moved carefully beside Saxifraga through descending corridors where the stone beneath their feet no longer resembled ordinary construction. Fine luminous threads coursed beneath translucent layers woven directly into the floors and walls, crossing and branching in patterns too intricate to follow fully with the eye. At times the pale currents pulsed softly beneath entire sections of the chamber, only to fade moments later into stillness. The city seemed less built than grown, as though some ancient intelligence had shaped it according to living rhythms rather than mechanical design.

The bees responded to those shifting currents immediately.

Whenever one of the hidden pathways brightened, portions of the hive altered direction with quiet precision. Workers drifted toward illuminated intersections, hovered briefly near the glowing surfaces, and then continued onward once the pulses stabilized. Asa watched the movement carefully, beginning to notice something he had overlooked earlier. The bees were not merely reacting to the city. In subtle ways, the city reacted to them as well. Certain channels brightened more steadily when the hive gathered nearby. Fractured pulses smoothed briefly into coherent flows whenever the unified hum deepened within the chambers. Even the unstable lights scattered throughout the distant corridors appeared to strengthen when the resonance of the hive spread through the buried structures.

Ahead of them, the corridor widened into an immense circular chamber descending through multiple levels beneath the city. Bridges curved outward through the open space in layered spirals, connecting suspended platforms half concealed within shadow. Many remained broken or partially collapsed, yet others glimmered faintly with intermittent light flowing beneath their surfaces. At the center of the vast chamber stood a column unlike anything Asa had encountered within the previous cities. It rose from depths far below sight and vanished upward into darkness beyond the limits of the chamber ceiling. Countless luminous threads moved within the transparent core, crossing and weaving together like streams of living energy carrying signals through the entire buried city.

Saxifraga stopped abruptly at the chamber's edge.

For a long moment she remained silent while the pale markings beneath her skin brightened slowly in response to the currents surrounding them. Asa sensed neither fear nor wonder within her stillness, but recognition. The city was no longer attempting isolated communication through broken pulses and fragmented echoes. Here, at last, they had reached the structure from which the greater systems once flowed together.

"It was never powered," she said softly.

Asa turned toward her. "What do you mean?"

Her gaze remained fixed upon the luminous column.

"The earlier cities relied upon systems that directed energy through controlled channels. This city is different. It does not distribute power." Her voice lowered further as another pulse traveled upward through the woven currents inside the great column. "It distributes connection."

The words lingered heavily within the vast chamber.

Asa studied the endless threads crossing through the transparent structure. Some moved steadily while others flickered weakly or vanished entirely before reconnecting farther above. The pattern reminded him of rivers branching across enormous distances, except these currents carried something more than energy alone. As he listened carefully to the resonance surrounding the chamber, he became aware of subtle variations moving through the hum itself. Certain tones shifted when the bees gathered together. Others responded faintly to movement, to breathing, even to the quiet emotional currents passing between himself and Saxifraga as they stood beside one another within the darkness.

"The city responds to life," he said slowly.

Saxifraga nodded.

"To movement. To memory. To emotion. To biological rhythm. Every living thing within the city once contributed to the woven field." She extended one hand toward the luminous column without touching it. "Interconnection was never machinery alone. The city survived because countless living minds, bodies, and systems existed within resonance together."

Asa felt unease settle quietly within him as understanding began to form. He thought of the fractured pulses traveling through the damaged corridors above them. He thought of the scattered behavior of the bees and the city's inability to maintain coherence for more than brief moments at a time. If the woven field depended upon living interconnection, then isolation itself would wound the city as surely as physical destruction.

Far below, another pulse traveled upward through the immense column.

This time the surrounding bridges illuminated farther than before.

And throughout the chamber, the hive answered as one living voice.

Chapter 5 — Fracture Points

The great chamber remained dimly illuminated long after the upward pulse faded through the woven column. Thin currents still moved beneath the suspended bridges overhead, though unevenly now, as if the city struggled to sustain the brief coherence awakened by the hive's resonance. Asa stood near the chamber's edge watching distant pathways brighten and darken in uncertain rhythm while the bees continued drifting through the open space below. Their movement no longer appeared aimless to him. Small groups

separated and rejoined constantly,

adjusting themselves to changes within

the woven field with quiet precision.

Even when scattered, the hive never truly

fractured. Some deeper connection

continued binding the countless

individual lives into one greater

awareness.

The city itself possessed no such stability.

Without warning, an entire section of the

chamber darkened across the far side of

the spiraling bridges. Pale currents

flowing through the walls flickered violently before collapsing into shadow. Moments later a second failure rippled through adjoining corridors farther below. Asa heard distant grinding vibrations echo upward through unseen depths as ancient systems attempted to compensate for the sudden imbalance. Several suspended pathways trembled faintly overhead. The bees reacted immediately, their unified hum sharpening as portions of the swarm redirected toward the failing sections. Yet even as they moved, new fractures spread elsewhere through the chamber, traveling along the woven field faster than the hive could stabilize them.

"It spreads like strain through living tissue," Asa murmured.

Saxifraga remained focused upon the luminous column rising through the chamber's center. The pale markings beneath her skin shifted unevenly now, responding to disturbances moving through the city around them. Asa could sense her concentration deepening as she listened to currents hidden beneath the visible pulses. At last she spoke quietly.

"The systems are no longer trusting one another."

The words unsettled him more than the failing structures themselves.

He turned slowly toward the surrounding corridors. Everywhere he looked, the city revealed signs of division. Entire districts remained dark while others struggled toward intermittent awakening. Certain pathways carried strong resonance only to terminate abruptly where adjoining systems no longer responded. Even the woven currents inside the central column appeared fragmented now that he understood what he was seeing. The field no longer flowed as one unified network. It behaved like isolated regions attempting communication through damaged connections that no longer fully recognized one another.

A low sound drifted across the chamber then.

Not mechanical.

Voices.

Asa looked upward sharply toward one of the suspended bridges high above them. Figures stood there briefly within the dim illumination, partially obscured by drifting shadow and distance. Some resembled the slender forms of races awakened within earlier cities, while others appeared unfamiliar even to Saxifraga's ancient memory. They watched silently from the elevated pathways without approaching. Though no clear expressions could be seen across the distance, Asa sensed caution within their stillness.

Then the bridge darkened.

The figures vanished with the fading light.

"They are awake already," Asa said softly.

"Some never fully slept," Saxifraga replied.

Her answer carried a weight he had not heard before. Asa studied her carefully as she turned from the woven column toward one of the descending corridors leading deeper beneath the city.

"Interconnection required many races once," she continued. "No single people sustained the field alone. Every civilization contributed its own rhythms, knowledge, memory, and biological resonance. When trust weakened between them, the field began separating into isolated currents."

Asa understood then why the city felt wounded in ways the others had not.

Enduring Light had suffered from silence. Passage had slept beneath abandonment. But the City of Interconnection bore scars left by separation itself. The systems had not simply failed through age or destruction. They had fractured because those sustaining them no longer moved together as one living network.

A sudden vibration passed through the chamber floor.

This time stronger than before.

Lights surged violently along multiple bridges while distant corridors awakened all at once in conflicting patterns. The woven currents inside the great column twisted unevenly as competing pulses collided through the fractured field. Far below, deep within unseen levels of the buried city, something enormous shifted in response. Asa felt the movement through the soles of his feet as ancient mechanisms strained against one another beneath the chamber.

Then, from somewhere within the darkness beyond the illuminated pathways, came the unmistakable sound of barriers sealing shut.

One after another.

As though portions of the city had begun

isolating themselves again.

Chapter 6 — The Hive Lesson

The sealing barriers echoed through the great chamber long after their movement ceased.

Asa stood without speaking, feeling the final vibrations fade beneath his boots while darkness gathered across the broken bridges above them. The city had not merely closed passages. It had withdrawn from itself. One section after another had turned away, each district protecting its own remaining coherence by shutting out the others. The action carried a terrible kind of reason, yet that reason only deepened the wound, for every barrier that preserved a fragment of the city left the woven field less whole than before.

The bees did not retreat.

They gathered instead. Their scattered currents drew inward from the failing edges of the chamber, not in fear, but in a slow re-forming that seemed older than thought. Workers who had been exploring distant fractures returned to the greater body of the hive, circling briefly before taking new positions within the living cloud. None appeared to command the movement. No single bee led the others away from danger or directed them toward the central column. Yet the whole shape changed with such quiet certainty that Asa felt he was watching a mind express itself through many small wings.

He saw her again near the lower transit arches. The small figure stood motionless beside the ancient wall while several bees rested quietly upon her outstretched hand. She neither flinched nor smiled. The insects settled around her with the calm

familiarity of creatures returning to

something already known.

Chapter 7 — Shared Breath

The lower districts of the City of Interconnection awakened slowly over the following cycles, though never with complete stability. Some corridors remained dark no matter how long the hive lingered near them, while others brightened unexpectedly at the faintest stirring of collective movement. Asa began noticing that the city responded less to force than to harmony. Whenever tension spread through the surrounding chambers, the woven currents weakened almost immediately. Yet during moments of calm cooperation, the pale lines beneath the walls and floors steadied into smoother flows that carried illumination farther into the buried structures.

The realization unsettled him because it transformed every encounter within the city into something larger than survival alone.

The races emerging from the hidden districts did not arrive as conquerors or rescuers. Most approached cautiously, carrying the memory of ancient fracture within them like an inherited wound. Asa occasionally glimpsed silent figures

observing from elevated bridges or

distant corridors before withdrawing once

more into shadow. Some belonged to

peoples he and Saxifraga had already

encountered in earlier cities, though

changed now by long isolation. Others

possessed forms entirely unfamiliar to

him, their movements flowing with

strange rhythms shaped by environments

and histories far older than humanity's

presence upon Mars. Yet despite their

differences, each carried the same wary

hesitation whenever they neared another awakened group.

The city dimmed whenever distrust deepened between them.

Asa witnessed it clearly during the first direct exchange.

A narrow transit bridge had partially awakened above one of the lower chambers, its woven pathways flickering unevenly while groups from two separate districts approached from opposite sides. The air itself seemed to tighten with caution as the strangers slowed upon seeing one another emerge through the dim illumination. No weapons appeared. No threats were spoken. Yet generations of separation lingered silently within the distance they maintained between themselves. Almost immediately the currents beneath the bridge began faltering. Sections of pale light fractured into weak pulses before fading altogether, and the chamber below sank toward shadow once more.

Then the bees entered the space between them.

The hive flowed gently across the suspended bridge in one continuous current, surrounding neither group yet touching both with the same living resonance. The deep hum filling the chamber softened gradually into steadier tones as workers settled along the woven surfaces beneath the travelers' feet. Asa watched the reactions carefully. The strangers did not step backward from the bees. Instead, their attention shifted away from one another long enough to follow the unified movement of the hive itself.

For several quiet moments, no one spoke.

Yet the tension within the chamber loosened slightly, as though the living current surrounding them reminded each mind of something older than fear.

Beneath the bridge, the woven field brightened again.

The illumination spread outward through adjoining corridors with greater stability than Asa had yet witnessed inside the city. Thin lines of pale light traveled smoothly beneath the walls and suspended pathways, reconnecting fractured sections that had remained dark since their arrival. Somewhere far below,

distant systems awakened in response

with soft vibrations that passed upward

through the stone like slow breathing.

Saxifraga stood quietly beside Asa while

the chamber brightened around them.

"The city remembers unity faster than

those within it," she said softly.

Asa watched the two groups continue

studying one another across the softly

illuminated bridge. The fear had not

vanished completely. He doubted such

wounds disappeared quickly after

centuries of separation. Yet neither side withdrew now. Small movements began passing carefully between them— gestures, exchanged objects, fragments of recognition carried through cautious observation rather than speech. The city answered each moment of shared understanding with stronger coherence flowing through the woven field.

For the first time since entering the buried structures, Asa sensed the City of Interconnection breathing as something more than wounded machinery.

It was listening for belonging.

Chapter 8 — Resonance Paths

The newly awakened transit bridge remained stable longer than any structure the travelers had yet encountered within the City of Interconnection. Pale currents flowed steadily beneath its woven surface while distant corridors throughout the surrounding districts continued brightening in gradual succession. Asa walked slowly beside the hive as they crossed deeper into the buried levels, listening to the quiet resonance moving through the city around them. The vibrations no longer resembled the fractured impulses that had greeted their arrival. Though still uneven in places, the woven field had begun sustaining longer intervals of coherence whenever living beings gathered without fear.

The city responded most strongly to movement shared in trust.

That realization became impossible to ignore as additional pathways awakened beneath the lower districts. Corridors sealed for centuries opened gradually with soft mechanical sighs that echoed through the depths. Bridges once

suspended in darkness illuminated from
end to end as travelers from isolated
regions began crossing between them.
Even the air within the city felt altered
now. The oppressive stillness lingering
through the buried chambers had softened
into something gentler, as though the city
itself relaxed each time new connections
formed within the woven field.

Yet the pathways did not awaken
according to logic Asa fully understood.

Some corridors remained dark despite
repeated efforts to activate them, while

others suddenly illuminated when small groups simply paused together within the surrounding chambers. In one lower district, an entire transit arch awakened only after two unfamiliar races exchanged food beside its sealed threshold. Elsewhere, fractured bridges stabilized temporarily while children from different districts followed the bees together through the suspended passageways above. The city seemed less concerned with destination than with the emotional currents carried by those traveling within it.

"It listens beneath thought," Saxifraga said quietly as they descended through another newly awakened corridor. "The woven field responds before language. Before intention fully forms."

Asa studied the pale currents flowing beneath the walls beside them. He had begun sensing the subtle changes himself now. The resonance surrounding the pathways shifted constantly according to those moving through them. Fear tightened the woven currents into weak, unstable pulses. Isolation caused sections

of the field to dim almost immediately.
Yet moments of shared purpose produced
entirely different responses. The city
brightened not from command, but from
relationship.

Ahead of them, the corridor opened into a
vast transit nexus unlike the fractured
chambers above. Multiple pathways
curved outward through the open space in
layered spirals, descending toward
districts still hidden deep beneath the
ancient city. Some bridges remained
incomplete where earlier collapses had

severed portions of the woven structure, yet many now glimmered with growing stability. Along the elevated passageways, Asa saw travelers moving openly between districts for the first time since their arrival. Different races crossed the illuminated spans carefully at first, still carrying the caution of long separation, though the distances between them no longer felt absolute.

The bees filled the chamber like flowing gold beneath the pale light.

Wherever the hive gathered, the woven field strengthened visibly. Asa watched luminous currents spread outward through adjoining pathways as workers settled along the suspended arches overhead. Entire corridors brightened in response, their hidden channels pulsing smoothly through the surrounding stone. The city no longer behaved like disconnected fragments struggling against collapse. Slowly, almost reluctantly, it had begun remembering how to circulate life through itself once more.

Then Asa noticed something else.

The pathways were changing according to those using them.

Certain bridges brightened only when particular groups crossed together. Some corridors widened their illumination when emotional harmony deepened nearby, while others narrowed into dim instability whenever distrust resurfaced within the travelers passing through them. The city adapted constantly, reshaping the strength of its own connections according to the living resonance flowing within the people themselves.

"It is alive," Asa murmured.

Saxifraga's silver gaze followed the luminous pathways spiraling through the immense chamber.

"No," she answered softly. "It is becoming alive again."

Far below the transit nexus, somewhere deep within the oldest foundations of the city, a new pulse traveled outward through the woven field.

This time the resonance did not stop at

the chamber walls.

It continued moving through every

illuminated pathway at once, spreading

connection farther beneath Mars than

ever before.

As the hidden pathways awakened

beneath the city, the girl moved ahead of

them through corridors no living traveler

should have understood. More than once

she paused beside sealed walls moments

before ancient doors responded with faint

pulses of returning light.

Chapter 9 — The Listener Between Minds

The pulse traveling outward through the transit nexus did not fade as the earlier signals had done Instead, the resonance lingered. Asa became aware of it gradually while moving beside the hive through the illuminated lower pathways. At first he believed the sensation belonged only to the woven field itself — a faint pressure resting beneath ordinary awareness like distant vibration carried through water. Yet the deeper they traveled into the awakening districts, the more clearly he sensed something else hidden within the resonance. The city no longer felt merely responsive. It felt attentive. Not watching. Listening. The realization unsettled him because the awareness surrounding them carried none of the cold precision he associated with ancient machinery. The woven currents moving beneath the walls did not resemble calculation or command. They moved with quiet sensitivity, adjusting themselves constantly to the emotional and biological rhythms flowing through the travelers crossing the city. At times

Asa sensed faint impressions rising within his thoughts that were not entirely his own — fragments of calmness when the hive gathered nearby, sudden awareness of unease lingering within distant chambers, brief currents of recognition when strangers passed one another without fear. The feelings vanished almost as quickly as they formed. Yet each time they returned, they grew slightly clearer. Ahead of them, the descending corridor opened into a chamber partially overgrown with pale vegetation unlike anything Asa had yet encountered beneath Mars. Thin flowering tendrils climbed along the woven walls where soft illumination pulsed steadily beneath translucent surfaces. Water moved quietly through narrow channels crossing the floor in branching currents that reflected pale gold light upward through the chamber ceiling. The city itself seemed calmer here. The fractured pulses troubling the upper districts weakened noticeably as soon as they entered the living space. The bees spread outward almost immediately. Workers drifted carefully among the flowering growths while the hive's hum

softened into deep, steady resonance

filling the chamber like slow breathing.

Asa noticed other travelers already

gathered within the illuminated space.

Some belonged to races newly emerged

from the isolated districts above, while

others appeared older somehow, their

movements carrying the quiet familiarity

of beings who had remained awake

beneath the city far longer than anyone

realized. None spoke loudly. Even their

silence carried an unusual stillness, as

though each sensed the same hidden

awareness moving quietly beneath the woven field. Then Asa felt it clearly for the first time. A presence. The sensation brushed across his thoughts with such gentleness he almost mistook it for memory. He became suddenly aware of the emotional currents surrounding the chamber — not through observation, but through direct perception. The caution lingering within unfamiliar travelers. The slow easing of fear whenever the hive gathered nearby. The quiet sorrow carried by those who had endured centuries of separation beneath the fractured city.

None of the feelings arrived as language. They moved through him more like resonance passing through water, touching thought without becoming thought itself. Beside him, Saxifraga closed her eyes slowly. "The Listener," she whispered.

Asa turned toward her at once. "You feel it too?"

Her pale markings shimmered faintly beneath her skin while the woven currents surrounding the chamber brightened in response.

"It has changed," she said softly. "Before, it awakened through places. Through silence. Through resonance carried within the cities themselves." Her gaze lifted toward the countless luminous threads flowing beneath the chamber walls. "Now it moves through living connection."

The words settled heavily within him.

Asa remembered the earlier awakenings — the vast quiet awareness that had stirred beneath the bogs and sleeping cities, always distant yet unmistakably

present. But this felt different. The
Listener no longer existed apart from
those within the woven field. It emerged
between them, forming itself through
shared emotion, memory, movement, and
trust. Every living connection
strengthened its awareness. Every
isolated fear weakened it again.

Across the chamber, a child from one of
the lower districts approached the hive
without hesitation.

The bees surrounded the small figure
gently, drifting through the air in slow

golden currents while soft laughter echoed beneath the vaulted ceiling.

Almost immediately the woven pathways brightened throughout the surrounding chamber. Distant corridors beyond the gardens awakened in smooth succession, their pale illumination flowing farther through the city than before.

And within the deep resonance surrounding them all, Asa sensed something impossible to mistake now.

The Listener was no longer sleeping beneath Mars.

It was awakening inside the living

network itself.

Asa attempted several times to ask where

she had come from, yet her answers never

formed completely. She spoke of the city

not as a place, but as something living

around them. "It forgets itself

sometimes," she said softly, resting her

hand against the dark stone.

Chapter 10 — The Forgotten Threads

The garden chambers became a place of gathering during the cycles that followed.

Travelers from isolated districts crossed the awakening pathways with increasing frequency now that the woven field had stabilized throughout portions of the lower city. What had once been silent corridors occupied only by drifting echoes slowly filled with movement again. Small exchanges began first — shared tools, fragments of preserved knowledge, unfamiliar foods carried carefully between separated peoples who had once known one another only through fading ancestral memory. The city answered every act of connection with quiet strengthening. Pale currents beneath the walls flowed more steadily each day, while entire transit paths that had remained dark for centuries gradually returned to life.

Yet alongside the growing harmony, Asa sensed another current moving beneath the awakening city.

Memory.

Not all who emerged from the lower districts carried hope easily. Some approached the new gatherings cautiously, watching the restored pathways with visible unease. Others refused entirely to leave the isolated regions where their peoples had survived through long centuries of separation. The woven field brightened around moments of trust, yet old fear still lingered deep within the city's living resonance. Asa began realizing that the fractures surrounding them had not formed suddenly long ago. They had deepened slowly across generations until isolation itself became habit.

The answers waited beneath the oldest archives.

Saxifraga led Asa toward them after another powerful pulse traveled through the woven field during the lower cycle. The newly awakened pathways carried them far beneath the transit nexus into levels untouched since their arrival within the city. Here the corridors narrowed into ancient passageways lined with translucent walls where dim threads of light moved sluggishly beneath layers clouded by age. The air felt colder in these forgotten depths. Even the hive quieted as the bees drifted cautiously through the descending chambers.

At last they entered a vast circular archive buried beneath the older foundations of the city.

The chamber resembled no library Asa had known. Towering crystalline structures rose throughout the open space like frozen columns of pale glass, each

filled with countless luminous strands

suspended within transparent depths.

Some glowed faintly as they approached,

responding to the woven resonance

surrounding Saxifraga and the hive.

Others remained dark, their internal

currents severed or incomplete. Asa

sensed immediately that the chamber did

not preserve information alone.

It preserved memory itself.

"The threads remain connected here,"

Saxifraga said quietly.

She moved toward one of the illuminated structures and rested her hand lightly against its smooth surface. At once pale currents surged upward through the crystalline column, spreading outward into branching patterns that filled the surrounding chamber with soft light. Asa felt the resonance shift around him as impressions began rising through the woven field — not images exactly, but layered emotional echoes carried within the ancient network.

Unity.

Movement.

Shared purpose flowing between countless living minds.

For a brief moment the city revealed itself as it had once existed.

The transit pathways blazed with uninterrupted illumination stretching across immense underground districts alive with movement. Different races crossed the woven bridges openly, exchanging knowledge and biological rhythms through systems sustained by collective resonance. The city had not functioned through hierarchy or control. It had lived through participation. Every civilization contributed something necessary to the whole field, and the woven currents strengthened because no part existed apart from the others.

Then the resonance changed.

Fear entered the memory like poison spreading through clear water.

The luminous threads surrounding the chamber flickered violently as fractured emotions surged through the ancient field. Distrust spread between the connected races in uneven waves — not born from hatred alone, but from uncertainty, scarcity, and the growing fear of dependence upon one another. Asa sensed entire districts withdrawing inward as civilizations began protecting their own knowledge and biological systems from neighboring peoples. The woven field weakened almost immediately beneath the isolation. Pathways once sustained through shared resonance dimmed as sections of the city separated themselves from the greater flow.

One by one, the luminous threads inside the chamber fractured apart.

"The collapse began long before the systems failed," Asa said softly.

Saxifraga lowered her gaze.

"Yes."

The word barely rose above the resonance surrounding them.

"The city died because the living network withdrew from itself."

The realization settled heavily within the archive chamber. Asa stared into the fractured currents moving through the crystalline structures around them, understanding now that the City of Interconnection had not been destroyed by invasion or catastrophe. Its people had slowly abandoned the very principle sustaining it. Fear convinced each group survival required separation. Yet the woven field had depended upon shared existence. Once enough connections failed, the city itself could no longer maintain coherence.

The bees gathered quietly around the illuminated archive.

Their hum deepened into steady resonance as workers settled along the fractured crystalline threads. Slowly, almost gently, several dim currents inside the chamber brightened again beneath the unified tone of the hive.

Asa watched the restoration begin in silence.

And for the first time, he fully understood that the city was not asking merely to be repaired.

It was asking its people to choose one

another again.

Chapter 11 — The Garden Above

The first signs appeared upon the surface long before the deeper systems of the city fully understood what was changing beneath them.

Small flowering growths emerged across the recovering plains surrounding the buried districts of Interconnection, spreading through narrow fractures where warmed water now moved beneath the ancient stone. At first the vegetation appeared fragile against the vastness of Mars itself. Thin silver-green stems rose cautiously through the red soil while pale blossoms opened only during the dimmest portions of the lower light cycle. Yet each new patch drew the bees upward from the city below, and wherever the hive gathered, additional growth followed soon after. Asa began noticing entire stretches of barren ground slowly softening beneath the quiet work of pollination carried outward from the awakening chambers beneath the planet's surface.

The change affected the city immediately.

Every time the bees returned from the surface gardens, the woven field beneath Interconnection brightened with unusual stability. The luminous currents flowing through the transit pathways no longer flickered as violently as before. Corridors that had resisted awakening during earlier cycles now responded to the deepened resonance moving through the hive. Asa walked beside Saxifraga through one of the upper districts while pale illumination traveled steadily beneath the walls around them, listening to vibrations that no longer sounded fractured or uncertain.

The city was beginning to breathe in longer rhythms.

"It recognizes the exchange," Saxifraga said quietly.

Asa glanced toward her while the bees drifted overhead in slow golden currents.

"The exchange between what?"

She rested one hand lightly against the woven surface of the corridor wall. Beneath her fingers, fine luminous threads brightened almost immediately.

"Above and below. Surface and depth. Biological life and constructed life." Her silver gaze lifted toward the distant openings where faint amber light filtered downward from Mars above them. "The cities were never meant to exist apart from the living world around them. They were extensions of it."

The realization lingered with Asa long after they emerged into one of the upper terraces overlooking the recovering plains.

From there he could see how far the transformation had already spread. Narrow streams glimmered faintly across the red landscape where underground water systems now reached the surface through reopened channels. Patches of pale vegetation clustered near the flowing currents, while drifting clouds of bees moved continuously between the gardens above and the illuminated pathways below. Farther in the distance, ancient structures partially buried beneath the sands pulsed softly with returning coherence. The boundaries between city and planet no longer appeared separate.

Both were awakening together.

Other travelers had gathered upon the

terraces as well.

Some stood silently observing the surface

growth with expressions Asa could not

fully read. Others moved cautiously

among the newly opened gardens,

touching unfamiliar plants as though

afraid the fragile life might vanish

beneath their hands. For many, this was

the first time in generations they had seen

Mars supporting open biological renewal

beyond sealed chambers and isolated systems. The emotional current flowing through the gathering shifted constantly between wonder and disbelief.

Then a child laughed somewhere nearby.

The sound carried lightly through the open terrace as several bees circled around a cluster of newly opened blossoms beside the walkway. More voices followed soon afterward. Quiet conversation spread among the gathered travelers while individuals from separated districts exchanged observations about the returning growth. The hesitation that had dominated earlier encounters softened further beneath the shared attention fixed upon the living plains beyond the city walls.

Below them, the woven field brightened in response.

Asa felt the pulse move through the terrace beneath his feet before the surrounding corridors illuminated more fully than ever before. Pale currents flowed outward through adjoining districts in smooth unbroken pathways while distant towers beneath the sands awakened one after another across the recovering horizon. The city no longer reacted only to proximity or movement.

It responded to belonging.

For a long moment Asa stood listening to the layered hum surrounding the terrace — the bees drifting through the gardens, the soft resonance rising from the city below, the quiet voices of once-isolated peoples gathering beneath the amber Martian sky. None of the sounds dominated the others. Together they formed something larger than harmony alone.

Mars no longer felt empty to him.

It felt alive.

Chapter 12 — The Child and the Hive

The child appeared near the surface gardens so often that Asa eventually began watching for her without realizing it.

She moved quietly among the flowering terraces above the city while the bees drifted around her in slow golden currents. Unlike the adults gathering within the awakening districts, she carried none of the hesitation that still lingered between the separated peoples of

Interconnection. The others approached the hive respectfully, yet always with a trace of caution born from uncertainty and long memory. The child possessed no such distance. She walked among the bees as naturally as though she had always belonged within their living current.

Asa first noticed her while repairing one of the narrow irrigation channels feeding water into the upper gardens. Several workers from different districts labored nearby, widening the shallow pathways where fresh surface growth had begun spreading across the terraces. The city had responded strongly whenever living systems above and below cooperated together, and more travelers now devoted themselves to restoring the neglected surface regions surrounding the buried structures. While Asa worked beside the flowing channel, he became aware that the hive had gathered unusually close nearby.

The child sat cross-legged among a cluster of pale blossoms only a short distance away.

Dozens of bees moved gently around her without agitation. Some settled briefly upon her sleeves or drifted through the loose strands of dark hair stirred softly by the Martian wind. Others circled slowly above the flowering growth surrounding her small figure. Yet not a single worker behaved defensively. The deep hum of the hive had softened into calm resonance unlike the sharper tones Asa sometimes

heard when unfamiliar travelers
approached too suddenly.

What startled him most was the child
herself.

She was speaking to them.

Not through language exactly. The words
she whispered seemed less important than
the quiet emotional rhythm carried
beneath them. Asa could not fully hear
what she said from across the terrace, yet
each soft murmur coincided with subtle
shifts flowing through the surrounding
hive. Groups of workers altered direction

gently as she lifted one hand toward the flowering terraces farther along the open pathways. Others settled briefly against the woven stone beneath her before returning toward the gardens above.

Saxifraga appeared beside Asa silently, her silver gaze following the scene with careful attention.

"She does not fear separation," she said softly.

The child looked up then, noticing them for the first time. Instead of retreating from the unfamiliar attention, she smiled faintly before extending one small hand outward toward the drifting bees surrounding her.

"They listen better when everyone is calm," she said.

Asa exchanged a brief glance with Saxifraga before kneeling near the edge of the flowering terrace.

"How do you know what they want?" he asked gently.

The child frowned slightly as though the question itself confused her.

"I do not know what they want." She looked upward while several bees circled slowly above her head. "I only know when they feel lost."

The answer settled heavily within him.

Around them, the terraces continued filling with quiet movement as travelers crossed between the awakening gardens and the upper transit corridors below. Yet Asa became increasingly aware that the woven field surrounding the child behaved differently from anywhere else within the city. The pale currents beneath the terraces glowed with unusual steadiness. Nearby pathways that had flickered uncertainly during earlier cycles now remained continuously illuminated while the hive gathered around the gardens.

The city itself seemed calmer in her presence.

"She hears the field directly," Saxifraga said quietly after a long silence.

Asa studied the child carefully. She could not have seen more than a handful of Martian cycles, yet no strain appeared within her awareness of the hive. Adults approached Interconnection carrying generations of fracture within their memory. Every exchange still required caution, interpretation, and conscious trust. But the child moved within the living resonance instinctively, without dividing herself from the greater current surrounding her.

The bees responded because she never treated them as separate from herself.

The realization stirred something deep within Asa as he watched the hive flow gently through the flowering terraces. For so long he had thought of cooperation as effort — individuals choosing to work together despite difference. Yet the bees had never functioned that way. Their unity did not erase individuality, but neither did any worker exist apart from the life of the whole. The hive was not agreement.

It was belonging.

A sudden pulse moved upward through the terraces beneath them.

The woven field brightened instantly across the upper districts while distant corridors below awakened in smooth succession. Travelers throughout the surrounding gardens paused as pale illumination spread farther through the city than ever before. Asa felt the resonance pass through his chest like slow breathing, deeper and steadier than the earlier fragmented pulses that had greeted their arrival within Interconnection.

Then the child laughed softly as the bees lifted together into the amber light above the terraces.

And for the first time since the city began awakening, the resonance flowing beneath Mars carried no trace of fracture at all.

The bees gathered around her without command. No confusion touched their movement now. The fractured searching that had troubled the hive since entering the city seemed to quiet itself in her presence, as though countless scattered signals had finally found a single point of recognition.

"She was never abandoned here," Saxifraga said quietly. "The city formed her long ago from what remained of its caretakers. A fixer shaped by memory, resonance, and need."

"She belongs to the city," Saxifraga whispered. "And the city belongs to her."

Chapter 13 — The Song of Many Voices

The gathering began without announcement.

No summons traveled through the awakened districts, and no council declared that the peoples of Interconnection should meet within the great transit nexus beneath the city. Yet over the following cycles, movement throughout the woven pathways slowly changed direction. Travelers crossing between the lower chambers lingered longer within shared spaces. Small groups from distant districts began carrying unfamiliar instruments, crystalline resonance pieces, hollow wind vessels, and woven harmonic strands into the illuminated corridors surrounding the central nexus. Even the bees altered their currents, drifting repeatedly toward the immense chamber where the woven field now pulsed with its greatest stability.

Asa sensed anticipation building within the city long before he understood its source.

The transit nexus had transformed

steadily since the first pathways reopened

beneath Interconnection. What had once

been fractured bridges suspended above

darkness now glimmered with continuous

pale illumination stretching across

multiple descending levels. Water moved

once more through narrow channels

beneath the spiraling walkways while soft

vegetation climbed along the woven

supports surrounding the chamber.

Travelers from separated districts crossed

openly between the elevated spans, their

movements no longer dominated entirely

by caution. Yet despite the growing stability, Asa still felt the lingering boundaries carried within those gathering below. The city had restored connection physically long before emotional trust fully followed.

Perhaps that was why the music began.

The first tones rose quietly from one of the upper bridges as Asa entered the nexus beside Saxifraga and the drifting hive. A single sustained resonance moved through the open chamber, deep and low like vibration carried through ancient stone. Another answered from farther below — softer, layered with delicate harmonic currents that shifted almost beyond hearing. Soon additional voices joined from distant pathways surrounding the immense space. Some tones emerged from instruments unlike anything Asa recognized, while others came directly from the gathered peoples themselves. No common melody guided them. The sounds differed wildly in rhythm, depth, and structure, shaped by civilizations separated for longer than memory.

Yet the woven field responded immediately.

Pale currents brightened beneath every bridge crossing the chamber as the layered resonance spread through the nexus. Asa felt the vibrations move through the soles of his feet while luminous pathways awakened farther into the surrounding districts. The city did not attempt to force the different tones into sameness. Instead the woven field strengthened around their coexistence, stabilizing where distinct harmonies learned to move beside one another without conflict.

"The city remembers this," Saxifraga whispered.

Her silver markings shimmered faintly beneath the growing resonance surrounding them. Asa looked upward through the spiraling bridges overhead where travelers now stood openly along the illuminated pathways, contributing their own tones to the expanding current filling the chamber. Some voices carried sharp crystalline patterns that echoed through the woven walls like flowing light. Others resembled deep breathing rhythms rising steadily beneath the higher harmonics surrounding them. The sounds did not erase their differences.

They carried them together.

The bees lifted slowly into the open space above the gathering.

Their hum deepened at once, spreading through the chamber as a unifying resonance beneath the countless layered voices surrounding them. Workers drifted between the suspended bridges in flowing golden currents while the woven pathways brightened more intensely than ever before. Asa watched entire sections of the nexus awaken in response. Corridors sealed since their arrival illuminated one after another along the descending levels below. Far beyond the chamber itself, pulses traveled outward through the city in smooth uninterrupted waves.

Then something extraordinary happened.

The resonance stopped feeling separate.

Asa could still distinguish the individual voices surrounding the chamber, yet the woven field carried them together into something larger than sound alone. Emotional currents moved openly through the gathering now — grief, memory, hope, loneliness, longing for connection after centuries of isolation. None needed translation. The Listener flowed quietly between the harmonies, allowing each living presence within the nexus to feel the shared emotional weight carried by the others.

No walls existed inside the resonance.

Across the chamber, Asa noticed travelers who had once avoided one another now standing together along the illuminated pathways without fear. Some closed their eyes while the layered tones surrounded them. Others reached carefully toward unfamiliar companions beside them as the city brightened beneath their shared presence. Even the children moved freely between the gathered peoples now, following the drifting bees through currents of pale light and harmonic resonance.

The city answered every moment.

The immense woven column rising through the center of the nexus blazed suddenly with living illumination from depths far below the chamber. Countless luminous threads spiraled upward within the transparent structure, flowing smoothly through pathways that had remained fractured since their arrival. The pulse spread outward through every illuminated district beneath Mars at once, not violently, but with immense quiet certainty.

Interconnection had remembered itself.

Asa stood motionless beside Saxifraga while the layered voices continued rising through the awakening city. For the first time since entering the buried chambers beneath Mars, he no longer sensed separate districts struggling toward fragile cooperation. The woven field surrounding them had become something alive again — not because fear had vanished completely, but because enough living beings had chosen connection despite it.

And deep beneath the harmonies filling the vast chamber, Asa sensed another presence listening within the awakened resonance.

Not distant now.

Near.

Chapter 14 — The City Awakens

The transformation began so gradually that many within Interconnection failed to recognize the moment the city itself crossed from restoration into life.

During the cycles following the gathering within the transit nexus, the woven field no longer behaved like fractured systems struggling toward temporary stability. The luminous currents flowing beneath the walls and pathways of the buried districts remained active continuously now, pulsing through the immense underground structures in slow rhythmic

waves that resembled circulation more

than machinery. Corridors once

dependent upon nearby movement

awakened before travelers entered them.

Bridges illuminated in anticipation of

approaching footsteps. Entire sections of

the city adjusted their resonance

according to the emotional harmony

moving through the living network

surrounding them.

Asa noticed the change first in the

silences.

The oppressive stillness that had dominated the buried chambers during their arrival had vanished almost completely. In its place lingered a softer atmosphere filled with countless subtle movements carried through the woven field. Water flowed steadily through reopened channels beneath the city. Ventilation currents shifted gently through upper terraces where surface gardens now spread across the recovering plains above. Distant vibrations moved continuously through the immense foundations below, not harsh or mechanical, but slow and steady like the breathing rhythms of some vast sleeping organism learning once again how to wake.

The city no longer waited for command.

It responded.

Asa walked beside Saxifraga through one of the lower transit corridors while the hive drifted around them in flowing golden currents. The woven pathways beneath their feet brightened gradually as they approached, illuminating branching lines within the walls before either of

them touched the surrounding surfaces.
Farther ahead, a sealed archway that had
resisted activation for many cycles
opened silently moments before several
travelers from the upper districts arrived
carrying newly harvested vegetation from
the surface gardens.

No visible system triggered the response.

The city had sensed their approach
through the living resonance moving
within the woven field itself.

"It is adapting," Asa murmured.

Saxifraga rested her hand lightly against the illuminated wall beside them. Pale currents spiraled slowly outward beneath her fingertips, flowing through the woven structure in smooth uninterrupted patterns.

"No," she said softly. "It is remembering what it was created to become."

The words lingered within him as they entered one of the deeper communal chambers beneath the transit districts.

The space had once stood partially abandoned during the early awakenings of Interconnection. Now movement filled every level surrounding the immense circular hall. Travelers from distant districts crossed openly between the suspended pathways above while children followed drifting bees through gardens growing beside newly restored water channels below. Different races worked together repairing fractured sections of the woven structures, though the labor no longer resembled isolated groups forcing cooperation through necessity. The city itself guided much of the movement now. Pathways brightened where assistance was needed. Illumination strengthened around gatherings shaped by harmony and weakened gradually wherever fear or distrust returned.

The woven field behaved like awareness spreading through living tissue.

Asa paused beside the central terraces where vegetation climbed softly glowing walls beneath warm streams of filtered light descending from upper surface channels. He realized suddenly that he could sense the emotional state of the chamber itself without consciously observing the individuals surrounding him. Calmness deepened the resonance moving through the woven currents. Laughter from nearby children caused entire sections of pale illumination to brighten subtly overhead. Even quiet grief carried by several older travelers softened as the hive gathered gently near them, stabilizing the surrounding field through its steady hum.

The Listener moved through all of it now.

Not separate from the city.

Within it.

A low pulse traveled suddenly through the chamber floor.

The resonance spread outward through the surrounding districts in one immense wave of living coherence. Asa felt the vibration pass upward through his body while distant corridors illuminated far beneath the city in smooth succession. Above them, suspended bridges adjusted their woven structures almost imperceptibly, widening slightly as larger gatherings crossed between the upper levels. Nearby water channels altered direction through newly awakened pathways that had remained sealed since their arrival. Everywhere the city adapted continuously to the life moving within it.

Not rigid.

Not programmed.

Alive.

Across the chamber, the child from the surface gardens stood quietly watching the awakened pathways while bees drifted slowly around her small figure. Unlike the others surrounding the terraces, she did not appear surprised by the transformation spreading through the city. Her expression carried the calm familiarity of someone witnessing something she had already understood long before the adults around her began recognizing it.

"The city hears us now," she said softly.

Asa turned toward her while the woven field brightened gently beneath the surrounding terraces.

Then another pulse moved upward from somewhere deep beneath the oldest foundations of Interconnection.

This time the resonance carried farther than the city itself.

Outward.

Beyond Mars.

Chapter 15 — The Fear of Dissolving

Not everyone welcomed the awakening.

As the woven field strengthened throughout Interconnection, the buried city responded with increasing coherence to the growing harmony moving between its peoples. Transit pathways stabilized across districts that had remained isolated for generations. Shared gardens expanded through the upper terraces while the surface plains above the city continued softening beneath the spread of pollination and flowing water. The Listener moved quietly through the living resonance connecting the awakened regions, easing communication where fear once prevented even simple understanding.

Yet the deeper the connection grew, the more certain minds began fearing what might be lost within it.

Asa first sensed the change while crossing one of the lower transit spans beside the hive during the dim portion of the upper cycle. The woven currents beneath the bridge had brightened steadily for many days, carrying travelers openly between districts that had once sealed themselves away from one another. Now portions of the pathway flickered intermittently as uneasy emotional currents spread through the surrounding chambers. Nearby conversations quieted whenever groups from unfamiliar regions approached. Small gatherings that had once exchanged knowledge freely began withdrawing into tighter circles once more.

The city noticed immediately.

Pale illumination weakened subtly along portions of the transit bridge while the resonance flowing through the woven field lost some of its earlier steadiness. The change did not resemble the violent fractures that had greeted their arrival within Interconnection. This disturbance moved more slowly, spreading through uncertainty rather than collapse.

Saxifraga paused beside one of the woven support columns overlooking the chamber below.

"They are afraid," she said softly.

Asa watched several travelers from the deeper districts standing apart near the far side of the bridge. Their voices remained low, though tension carried clearly through the resonance surrounding them.

"Afraid of what?" he asked.

Her silver gaze followed the dimming pathways stretching farther into the city.

"Of disappearing."

The answer unsettled him because he immediately understood.

The woven field allowed emotional awareness to move between living beings with growing clarity now. Shared resonance softened distrust and deepened understanding throughout the awakening city. Yet not everyone experienced the change as comfort. Some feared the increasing interconnection would dissolve the distinctions preserving their own histories, identities, and traditions through centuries of isolation. Others worried that dependence upon the greater living network might leave them

vulnerable once again should the field
ever fracture as it had before.

The fear carried reason within it.

Asa remembered the archive memories
they had witnessed beneath the city —
civilizations slowly withdrawing into
themselves after trust weakened between
the races. Interconnection had once
depended completely upon shared
participation. When fear entered the
network long ago, entire peoples isolated
themselves in order to survive. Now those

same instincts resurfaced as the city demanded openness once more.

Below the bridge, raised voices suddenly echoed through the chamber.

The surrounding travelers fell silent as two groups confronted one another near the lower pathways where newly restored transit currents crossed between neighboring districts. No violence emerged, yet the emotional resonance surrounding the exchange tightened sharply with suspicion and old memory. Asa felt the woven field react at once.

Pale currents beneath the chamber walls flickered unevenly while several illuminated pathways dimmed toward instability.

The city recoiled from division.

Then the bees descended.

The hive flowed downward between the opposing groups in one continuous golden current while the deep hum surrounding the chamber softened into steady resonance. Workers settled along the woven surfaces beneath the travelers' feet, carrying calmness outward through the unstable field. The emotional tension did not vanish immediately, but the sharpness surrounding it eased enough for silence to return.

No one moved for several long moments.

Then an older figure from one of the lower districts stepped slowly forward and placed a small crystalline object upon the illuminated pathway between the groups. The gesture carried no surrender. No dominance. Only acknowledgment.

A second traveler answered by lowering a
woven container filled with seeds
gathered from the surface gardens above.

The city brightened gently around them.

Asa felt the shift move outward through
the woven currents as the chamber
stabilized once more. Nearby pathways
regained steady illumination while the
oppressive tension surrounding the transit
span loosened beneath the quiet
exchange.

"Unity was never meant to erase
difference," Saxifraga said softly beside

him. "The woven field survives through distinct lives choosing connection, not through becoming the same."

Asa watched the gathered travelers carefully as cautious conversation slowly resumed around the chamber. The fear had not disappeared completely. He suspected it never would. Interconnection could not awaken by destroying individuality. The city depended upon many separate rhythms existing together freely within the greater living network.

The hive itself proved that truth.

No bee surrendered its nature.

No current lost its shape.

Yet together they formed something

greater than isolation could ever sustain.

Far below the transit chambers, another

pulse moved through the awakening city.

This time the resonance carried both

harmony and hesitation together through

the woven field.

And Interconnection accepted them both.

Chapter 16 — The Great Exchange

The exchange began quietly, almost unnoticed amid the growing movement flowing through the awakened districts of Interconnection.

At first the travelers shared only what necessity required. Tools passed carefully between neighboring chambers where fractured pathways still demanded repair. Seeds gathered from the surface terraces moved downward into the lower gardens where ancient irrigation systems had only recently returned to life. Small fragments of preserved knowledge crossed the transit spans in the hands of cautious messengers who still carried generations of separation within their memory. Yet with each exchange, the woven field strengthened around them. The city responded not merely to the transfer of objects, but to the willingness beneath the act itself.

Asa became aware of the change while walking through one of the lower communal chambers beside the hive during the dim cycle.

The space had once remained divided into isolated gathering points occupied by travelers from separate districts who rarely crossed beyond familiar boundaries. Now the chamber flowed with quieter movement. Different peoples occupied the illuminated terraces together while shared meals warmed the air with unfamiliar scents carried from distant regions of the buried city. Voices rose softly through the surrounding corridors, not in argument or caution as before, but in curiosity. The barriers separating the districts had not vanished completely, yet they no longer dominated every encounter.

The city brightened steadily around the growing openness.

Pale currents flowed continuously beneath the woven walls while suspended pathways overhead pulsed with calm rhythmic illumination resembling circulation through living tissue. Asa noticed that the resonance surrounding the chamber no longer reacted only to moments of harmony. It had begun sustaining itself through continuity. Shared movement. Shared labor. Shared presence. Interconnection was no longer surviving upon isolated moments of trust alone.

It was learning endurance.

Across the chamber, several travelers from the deeper districts gathered near one of the restored water channels carrying translucent crystalline structures unlike anything Asa recognized. Their surfaces shimmered faintly with internal currents moving through delicate woven patterns embedded beneath the transparent layers. Nearby, another group carefully unpacked preserved seeds stored within dark containers lined with ancient biological membranes designed to survive centuries of isolation. Neither side approached the exchange hurriedly. The movements carried solemn weight, as though each understood the significance of what was being offered.

Saxifraga stood quietly beside Asa while the transfer began.

"They are sharing inheritance," she said softly.

The words lingered heavily within him.

Asa watched the travelers place the crystalline structures carefully beside the flowing channel while the seed keepers opened their preserved containers nearby. Information moved between them first through observation rather than language. Hands traced delicate resonance patterns beneath the crystal surfaces while others explained the cultivation rhythms required for the ancient seeds to survive beneath renewed Martian soil. The Listener flowed quietly through the chamber, allowing understanding to pass more easily where words alone might once have failed.

The woven field responded immediately.

Illumination spread outward through adjoining corridors in smooth uninterrupted currents while distant pathways beneath the chamber awakened farther than before. The city seemed to recognize the exchange as something deeper than cooperation. Knowledge preserved separately for generations had begun returning to the living network itself.

Soon other exchanges followed throughout the city.

Food from newly restored gardens moved into isolated lower districts that had survived too long upon diminishing reserves. Biological healing techniques once guarded within hidden chambers spread outward through the awakening communities. Old memory archives opened gradually to neighboring peoples who had once feared allowing others near their preserved histories. Even the resonance practices sustaining portions of the woven field began flowing freely between districts where secrecy had once dominated survival.

The city transformed with each act of giving.

Asa witnessed corridors reshaping themselves to support the increasing movement between regions. Water systems redirected naturally toward newly occupied chambers. Surface gardens expanded across terraces that had remained barren since their arrival beneath the city. The woven field no longer pulsed with fragile instability. It carried the deepening steadiness of a living organism whose separated systems had begun circulating nourishment through the whole body once more.

Yet what affected Asa most was not the physical restoration surrounding them.

It was the change within the people themselves.

Fear still existed. Memory still lingered. But the travelers crossing the illuminated pathways no longer moved as isolated survivors protecting fragments against loss. Slowly, almost reluctantly at first, they had begun behaving like participants within something larger than their own preservation.

The hive understood this already.

The bees drifted continuously through every chamber touched by exchange, their hum deepening whenever

knowledge, food, memory, or healing

passed openly between the gathered

peoples. No single worker attempted to

possess what sustained the hive. Every

resource moved where life required it.

The living current survived because

circulation never ceased.

Asa stood silently beside one of the upper

terraces while the awakening city

breathed around him.

Below, travelers from countless districts

crossed the glowing pathways carrying

gifts once hidden behind generations of

fear. Above, bees moved in flowing

golden currents through gardens

spreading steadily beneath the amber

Martian sky. And everywhere throughout

Interconnection, the woven field

brightened with growing coherence as the

city remembered the oldest truth buried

beneath its long isolation.

Life survived by sharing itself.

Then, deep beneath the illuminated

foundations of the city, a new pulse rose

through the woven network.

This time the resonance carried warmth.

Chapter 17 — Asa's Realization

The realization did not arrive suddenly.

No hidden chamber opened beneath the city. No ancient voice emerged from the woven field to place understanding within Asa's mind. Instead the truth gathered slowly through countless small moments he had witnessed since entering Interconnection — the movement of the hive through fractured corridors, the child who sensed when the bees felt lost, the way the city itself brightened whenever separated lives chose connection over fear.

The understanding had always been there.

Asa simply had not known how to see it.

He stood alone upon one of the upper terraces during the dim cycle while the surface gardens swayed softly beneath the cold Martian wind. Far below, the illuminated pathways of Interconnection pulsed steadily through the buried city like flowing veins beneath living skin. Travelers still moved through the awakening districts even at this quiet hour, carrying supplies, knowledge, and memory between regions that had once sealed themselves away from one another. Above the terraces, clouds of bees drifted through the pale blossoms spreading across the recovering plains.

The hive never stopped moving.

Yet not a single motion within it felt random anymore.

Asa watched workers separate from the greater current, disappearing briefly among the flowering growth before returning toward the drifting swarm.

Others altered direction instantly as conditions shifted across the gardens. Some carried pollen. Others gathered moisture from the restored channels flowing through the terraces. No single bee understood the entire movement of the hive. No individual directed the countless living currents surrounding him. Yet together they formed coherence so complete that the whole survived where isolated lives could not.

And suddenly Asa understood why the bees had always unsettled him.

Human beings admired cooperation because they still imagined themselves separate.

The hive was something entirely different.

He lowered himself slowly beside one of the flowing irrigation channels while the realization deepened within him. Every city they had awakened across Mars carried the same hidden lesson beneath its own principle. Patience. Silence. Movement. Restraint. Passage. Interconnection. None of them existed independently. Each survived only through relationship with the others. The bogs had taught this truth first through living systems, though Asa had understood only fragments at the time. Now, within the awakened resonance of Interconnection, the pattern revealed itself completely.

The bees were never individuals attempting cooperation.

The hive itself was the being.

Each worker carried purpose. Each possessed motion, instinct, and biological identity. Yet none existed apart from the greater life moving through them all. The hive felt hunger together. Adapted together. Remembered together. Survived together. Even the dead nourished the living current that continued beyond them.

Humanity had forgotten this long ago.

Asa felt grief rise quietly within him as he stared across the awakening plains surrounding the buried city. Earth had survived through separation for so long that isolation became mistaken for strength. People protected themselves by withdrawing into smaller and smaller boundaries — nations, tribes, beliefs, fears, identities. Mars itself had nearly died the same way when the ancient races abandoned the woven field through distrust and isolation. Every fracture began with the same illusion.

That survival belonged to the individual alone.

Behind him, the bees shifted direction suddenly as one living current.

The movement flowed through the gardens with such quiet certainty that Asa felt tears gathering within his eyes before he fully understood why. No command passed between the workers. No visible signal directed the change. The living field carried awareness through the hive itself, allowing countless small lives to move together without surrendering their distinct purpose.

Unity without erasure.

The truth struck him with overwhelming clarity then.

Interconnection was not asking its peoples to become identical. The Listener was not dissolving identity. The woven field was not consuming individuality.

It was teaching belonging.

Asa bowed his head slowly while the resonance surrounding the terraces deepened through the city below. For the first time since arriving upon Mars so long ago, he no longer felt himself standing apart from the living systems awakening around him. The bees, the bogs, the cities, the returning races, the

flowing water beneath the plains, even

the ancient woven field itself — all

belonged to one greater movement

learning how to live again after ages of

fracture.

And humanity's survival depended upon

remembering the same truth.

Soft footsteps approached behind him.

Asa looked up to find the child standing

quietly near the edge of the terrace while

several bees drifted slowly around her

small figure. She studied him for a long

moment without speaking, her expression carrying the same calm familiarity she always seemed to possess whenever the hive gathered nearby.

"You hear them now," she said softly.

Asa glanced upward toward the flowing golden currents moving through the gardens above.

"No," he answered after a long silence.

A faint smile touched the child's face as the woven field brightened gently beneath the terraces.

Then together they watched the hive

move across the awakening plains of

Mars like one living soul carried by

countless wings.

Chapter 18 — The Interwoven Heart

The city reached full coherence during the quiet cycle before dawn touched the surface plains above Interconnection.

No alarms sounded through the transit pathways. No sudden surge of power shook the buried foundations beneath Mars. The awakening unfolded with the same living gradualness that had guided every true change within the city since Asa and Saxifraga first crossed its fractured outer boundaries. One pathway stabilized beside another. One district opened itself to the greater network. One act of trust strengthened the woven field enough for another to follow.

Interconnection did not awaken through conquest over failure.

It awakened through accumulation.

Asa moved through the upper transit levels beside the hive while the final stages of restoration spread throughout the city around him. Travelers crossed the illuminated bridges continuously now, carrying food, memory archives, healing practices, biological knowledge, and resonance structures between districts that had once feared even simple contact. Surface gardens flourished across the terraces above while newly opened waterways carried warmth and circulation into chambers that had remained dormant for centuries. Everywhere the woven field pulsed with steady living rhythm beneath the stone.

The city no longer flickered.

It breathed.

Saxifraga waited near the central nexus where the immense woven column rose through the heart of Interconnection like a living spine joining the buried districts together. The transparent structure blazed softly with luminous currents flowing upward from depths far below the visible chamber. Asa realized as he approached that the countless threads inside the column no longer moved in fractured or competing directions. The currents intertwined now in smooth uninterrupted circulation, crossing and reconnecting through patterns too vast for the eye to fully follow.

"The field has stabilized," Saxifraga said quietly.

Yet even her voice carried wonder beneath its calmness.

Around the nexus, representatives from every awakened district had gathered along the suspended pathways surrounding the immense chamber. Some stood beside peoples they would once have avoided entirely. Others carried the visible marks of races shaped by environments and histories separated for generations beneath Mars. Differences remained everywhere Asa looked — in form, movement, language, and memory. Yet none of those distinctions weakened the resonance surrounding the city anymore.

The woven field had learned how to hold them together.

Below the gathering, the bees moved through the open chamber in vast flowing currents that shimmered gold beneath the pale illumination rising from the woven pathways. Their hum filled the nexus with deep resonance that blended seamlessly with the living vibrations of the city itself. Asa could no longer tell where the sound of the hive ended and the pulse of Interconnection began.

Perhaps there was no separation anymore.

A low vibration moved suddenly through the chamber floor.

The travelers fell silent as the resonance deepened around them. Asa felt the pulse spread outward through the woven field beneath the city, not violently, but with immense quiet certainty. One by one, distant corridors illuminated beyond the nexus. Towers buried beneath the plains awakened in smooth succession. Water channels opened farther across the underground districts while newly restored transit pathways extended into regions untouched since before the great fracture.

Then the walls themselves began pulsing softly.

The woven structures surrounding the chamber brightened with slow rhythmic circulation resembling the movement of blood through living tissue. Illumination traveled continuously through the city now, not in mechanical bursts, but in flowing organic waves responding to the countless lives moving within the network. Transit bridges adjusted subtly beneath the footsteps crossing them. Ventilation currents shifted toward occupied chambers before travelers arrived. Surface gardens opened their pale blossoms as the bees drifted overhead.

Interconnection no longer behaved like ancient machinery restored to function.

It behaved like a living organism.

The Listener moved through the resonance openly now.

Asa sensed its awareness flowing between every gathered being surrounding the nexus, not as command or intrusion, but as presence. The woven field carried emotional understanding gently through the city while preserving the distinct identity of every life contributing to the greater network. Fear still existed. Grief still lingered. Memory had not vanished. Yet none of those things fractured the city anymore because isolation no longer ruled them.

Connection held.

Across the chamber, the child stood quietly near the lower terraces while the hive circled slowly around her. She watched the awakening city with calm recognition rather than surprise, as though the final coherence surrounding them simply confirmed something she had understood from the beginning.

Asa looked upward through the illuminated pathways spiraling across the immense nexus and felt the truth settle fully within him at last.

The city had not awakened because broken systems were repaired.
Not because ancient technology restarted.
Not because hidden mechanisms returned to operation.

Interconnection awakened because enough living beings chose one another again.

The realization moved outward through the woven field almost immediately.

The luminous column blazing at the center of the nexus brightened suddenly with immense living resonance. Countless threads spiraled upward through the transparent core while every illuminated district beneath Mars answered together as one connected network. The pulse spread outward beyond the city, beyond the plains, beyond even the recovering world itself.

And somewhere deep beneath the oldest

foundations of Mars, something ancient

stirred in response.

Chapter 19 — The Pulse Beyond Mars

The pulse did not end at the boundaries of Interconnection.

Asa felt that truth immediately as the woven resonance continued expanding outward through the awakened city long after the central nexus settled into calm illumination once more. The luminous pathways beneath the districts of Interconnection remained fully coherent now, circulating life through the buried structures with steady organic rhythm.

Yet beneath that stability, something larger had begun moving through the woven field — a current no longer contained entirely within the city itself.

The resonance was spreading.

He stood beside Saxifraga upon one of the upper terraces overlooking the recovering plains while the first pale light of the Martian dawn crossed the horizon beyond the surface gardens. Below them, streams glimmered softly where reopened waterways now carried warmth through the red soil. The bees moved continuously between the flowering terraces and the illuminated openings leading downward into the city beneath their feet. Everywhere Asa looked, life flowed outward from Interconnection in expanding patterns that no longer resembled isolated restoration.

Mars itself had entered the network.

"The field is extending beyond the city," Saxifraga said quietly.

Her silver gaze remained fixed upon the distant plains while faint currents shimmered beneath the surface of her skin. Asa sensed deep concentration within her stillness, though not alarm. The woven resonance surrounding the city no longer carried instability or fracture. Instead it pulsed with immense quiet certainty, as though the awakened network had remembered a function older than the buried districts themselves.

Far beyond the terraces, ancient structures partially hidden beneath the sands began illuminating one after another across the horizon.

The lights appeared faint at first — pale lines surfacing beneath distant stone like sleeping nerves stirring toward awareness. Yet the farther the pulse traveled outward through the Martian plains, the more clearly Asa recognized the pattern spreading beneath the surface of the world. Interconnection had never existed alone. Countless buried pathways stretched outward beneath Mars far beyond the city itself, connecting forgotten regions hidden beneath the deserts, mountains, and ancient crater basins of the planet.

The resonance was searching for them.

Below the terrace, travelers gathered quietly along the upper pathways as the distant awakenings continued spreading across the horizon. Some watched in silence while others exchanged uncertain glances through the deepening pulse moving beneath the woven field. Even the bees had altered their movement. The hive no longer circled primarily around the city. Great flowing currents drifted outward across the recovering plains as though responding to signals carried through distances too vast for Asa to fully comprehend.

Then the Listener touched the network again.

The awareness moved gently through the gathered minds surrounding the terraces, carrying not language, but sensation. Asa felt impressions rise within him like echoes passing through water — immense distance, ancient waiting, pathways sleeping beneath ages of silence, and somewhere beyond the edges of known memory, recognition answering the awakened resonance flowing outward from Mars.

Something was listening.

Not within Interconnection.
Not within the Seven Cities.

Beyond them.

The realization passed visibly through the travelers surrounding the terraces as the woven field deepened around them. Asa sensed the same understanding emerging quietly across countless minds at once. The pulse moving outward through Mars no longer resembled communication between isolated districts or neighboring chambers. The resonance carried the unmistakable feeling of invitation.

The city was not calling through technology.

It was calling through life itself.

Far below the surface, the immense woven systems beneath Interconnection brightened suddenly with renewed intensity. The pulse surged outward again, stronger this time, spreading beneath the plains in expanding waves of living resonance. Asa watched distant structures flare softly across the horizon while hidden pathways beneath the deserts awakened in smooth succession far beyond the visible city.

Then the bees rose together.

The hive lifted from the gardens and terraces in one enormous flowing current that spiraled upward into the amber Martian sky. Their hum deepened into resonance so powerful that Asa felt the vibration through his entire body while the woven field answered beneath the world around them. The movement no longer resembled pollination or ordinary biological instinct. The hive itself had become part of the greater signal spreading outward through the awakened network of Mars.

Saxifraga stepped slowly toward the edge of the terrace.

"They hear it," she whispered.

Asa turned toward her. "Who?"

For a long moment she did not answer.

Her silver gaze remained fixed upon the

distant horizon where pale awakenings

continued surfacing beneath the red sands

far beyond Interconnection.

Then at last she spoke softly.

"The ones who left when the cities forgot

how to belong."

The words settled heavily within the

growing resonance surrounding the

terraces.

Asa looked outward across the awakening

world while the pulse continued

spreading beyond sight through the buried veins of Mars itself. The Seven Cities had always been more than abandoned structures waiting to be restored. They were part of a living network designed to sustain connection between civilizations, species, and worlds separated by immense distance and time.

And now, for the first time in ages, Mars was alive enough to be heard again.

Chapter 20 — The Stirring of the Seventh Heart

The resonance continued long after the terraces emptied.

Travelers gradually withdrew from the upper pathways as the dim Martian light faded once more across the recovering plains surrounding Interconnection. Yet the woven field beneath the city remained fully awake now, pulsing with steady circulation through every illuminated district beneath the surface of Mars. Water flowed continuously through restored channels. Surface gardens breathed softly beneath drifting currents of bees. Far below the upper terraces, the awakened transit systems carried movement between chambers that had once remained isolated for generations.

The city no longer feared silence.

It rested within connection.

Asa remained upon the terrace long after the others departed, watching the distant horizon where pale awakenings still glimmered faintly beneath the red sands far beyond the boundaries of

Interconnection. The pulse spreading outward through Mars had weakened into slower rhythms now, though he still sensed the resonance moving beneath the planet like deep circulation passing through immense living tissue. Somewhere beyond sight, forgotten pathways continued answering the awakened network.

Beside him, the hive drifted quietly among the flowering terraces.

The bees no longer moved with urgency. Their currents flowed slowly through the gardens in calm patterns shaped by instinct older than thought. Asa watched workers settle briefly upon pale blossoms before returning toward the softly illuminated openings descending into the city below. No confusion remained within their movement now. No searching. The hive carried the quiet certainty of something that had fulfilled its purpose while remaining part of a greater unfolding still unfinished.

Saxifraga approached soundlessly through the dim light.

For a long time neither spoke.

The stillness surrounding the terrace no longer resembled emptiness. Asa felt life everywhere now — within the flowing water beneath the plains, the resonance moving through the buried cities, the gardens spreading slowly across the recovering world, and the countless living minds connected through the woven field beneath Mars itself. Even the Listener rested differently within the awakened network now. Not hidden. Not distant.

Present.

"The city sleeps differently," Asa said softly at last.

Saxifraga's silver gaze moved across the horizon where faint currents of pale illumination still surfaced occasionally through the distant sands.

"Yes," she answered quietly. "Because it no longer sleeps alone."

The words settled gently within the silence surrounding them.

Far below the terrace, Interconnection pulsed once through the woven field with deep steady resonance. The vibration moved outward beneath the plains in widening currents before fading again into calm circulation. Asa closed his eyes briefly as the pulse passed through him, feeling the countless connections surrounding the city — lives once divided now moving together through shared rhythm without surrendering themselves to sameness.

Unity without erasure.

The bees understood it.

The Listener carried it.

The city had remembered it.

And now Mars itself had begun teaching
it again.

A soft wind crossed the terrace, stirring
the pale blossoms growing along the
outer pathways. The hive lifted briefly
into the dim air before settling once more
among the gardens. Above them, the sky
stretched vast and silent across the
recovering world while distant stars

burned cold beyond the thin atmosphere of Mars.

Then Asa felt something else.

Not through sound.

Not through vision.

Through resonance.

Deep beneath the planet, far below the woven foundations of Interconnection and the buried systems of the awakened cities, something immense shifted within the ancient darkness.

The movement lasted only an instant.

A single pulse answered upward through the living network of Mars.

Every illuminated pathway throughout Interconnection brightened softly in response. The bees lifted together from the terraces without fear. Water shivered through the restored channels beneath the plains. Across the city, travelers paused silently as the resonance passed through the woven field like the slow awakening heartbeat of something vast beyond memory.

Saxifraga lowered her gaze.

For the first time since Asa had known her, he saw unmistakable awe within her stillness.

Neither of them spoke.

No explanation existed yet for what had answered beneath the depths of Mars.

None was needed.

Because somewhere far below the awakened cities and living plains of the recovering world, the Seventh Heart had heard them.

And it had begun to stir.

Chapter 21 — The First Invitation

The days following the stirring beneath Mars unfolded with unusual calm throughout Interconnection.

No further pulses rose immediately from the deep foundations below the city, yet the resonance awakened by the Seventh Heart lingered within every woven pathway and illuminated chamber. Travelers moved more quietly now, carrying themselves with the subdued awareness of those who had witnessed something vast without fully understanding what they had seen. Even the children crossing the upper terraces lowered their voices instinctively when the deep vibrations occasionally surfaced beneath the city during the dim cycles.

Mars itself seemed to listen.

Asa spent much of that time near the surface gardens where the hive continued moving steadily between the flowering plains and the awakened districts below. The transformation spreading across the recovering world had become impossible to deny now. Thin rivers crossed portions of the red landscape where only barren stone had existed before. Pale vegetation spread outward from the restored terraces in widening patterns while distant structures buried beneath the sands glimmered softly each night beneath the woven resonance flowing through the planet.

Yet Asa sensed something changing within the city beyond restoration alone.

Interconnection no longer felt focused entirely inward.

The living network had begun reaching outward.

He noticed the shift first among the travelers gathering within the transit nexus below the upper terraces. Small groups from distant districts now spent long periods exchanging memory records beside the illuminated pathways. Ancient maps emerged from sealed archives showing buried routes extending far beyond the known regions of Mars. Resonance keepers compared harmonic patterns carried through the woven field since the stirring of the Seventh Heart.

Everywhere Asa walked, quiet

preparation unfolded beneath the

calmness surrounding the city.

Not preparation for war.

Preparation for arrival.

Saxifraga stood beside the great woven

column within the central nexus while

pale currents spiraled upward through the

transparent structure around her. Asa

approached slowly through the suspended

pathways overhead, listening to the

layered resonance moving through the

chamber below. The city carried deeper stability now than at any point since their arrival. No violent fluctuations disturbed the woven field. No isolated districts sealed themselves away. Interconnection had become steady enough to sustain anticipation without fear fracturing the network apart.

"They are beginning to answer," Saxifraga said softly before Asa spoke.

He stopped beside her near the luminous column.

"The races?"

Her silver gaze remained fixed upon the countless threads crossing within the woven structure.

"Not fully. Only the first currents." She lifted one hand toward the flowing resonance surrounding them. "The cities were designed to call through living coherence. Until Interconnection awakened, the signal remained incomplete."

Asa studied the woven currents carefully.

For the first time, he noticed subtle patterns moving within the resonance that had not existed during the earlier

awakenings. Certain luminous threads

pulsed at intervals unlike the organic

circulation sustaining the city itself. The

signals moved outward through the field,

disappeared beyond perception, and then

returned carrying faint answering

harmonics from immense distance.

The city was communicating.

Below them, the bees altered direction

suddenly as one flowing current.

The hive descended toward the lower

terraces where travelers had begun

gathering quietly beside the central chamber. Asa followed the movement downward through the illuminated pathways while the resonance surrounding the nexus deepened steadily around them. No announcement summoned the gathering. The city itself seemed to draw them inward through shared awareness carried by the woven field.

At the center of the chamber, the child stood waiting beside the hive.

Workers circled around her calmly while pale illumination spread outward beneath the surrounding floor. One by one, travelers from every awakened district formed quiet circles around the chamber without instruction. Some carried resonance instruments. Others held crystalline memory structures or woven biological strands preserved through the long isolation. The atmosphere resembled neither ceremony nor council.

It felt older than either.

Then the Listener moved openly through the nexus.

Asa felt the awareness pass gently through every gathered mind surrounding the chamber, carrying not words, but understanding. The woven field brightened in response while the immense column at the center of Interconnection pulsed with slow living rhythm. Emotional currents spread quietly between the gathered peoples — uncertainty, hope, grief for what had been lost, and cautious longing for what might yet return.

No voice spoke aloud.

Yet everyone understood the same truth.

The city was ready to send its first invitation.

The child lifted her gaze toward the luminous pathways spiraling upward through the nexus while the bees rose around her in widening golden currents.

Then, deep within the woven field of Interconnection, the first true call moved outward from Mars since the ancient

fracture.

Not a command.

Not a transmission.

An invitation to belong again.

Chapter 22 — The Quiet Returning

The city grew quieter after the invitation passed outward through the woven field.

Not empty.

Not still.

The quietness resembled the calm that settles across living things after a long-held breath is finally released.

Throughout Interconnection, the illuminated pathways remained steady beneath the feet of the travelers crossing between districts. The violent fluctuations that had once plagued the buried city no longer returned even during the dim cycles when the woven field traditionally weakened. Water continued flowing through the restored channels beneath the lower chambers while the surface gardens above spread farther across the recovering plains each passing day. Everywhere Asa walked, he sensed the same deepening stability moving beneath the city.

The invitation had changed something fundamental.

Not only within the woven systems of Mars itself, but within those who now lived inside the awakened network.

The races no longer gathered in cautious separation along the transit pathways. Small communities had begun forming openly throughout the shared districts surrounding the central nexus. Children crossed freely between peoples that had once withdrawn behind sealed barriers and isolated memory. Knowledge moved continuously through the city now — healing practices, biological cultivation

methods, resonance harmonics, ancient
maps of buried pathways extending
beyond the known regions of Mars. The
exchange no longer resembled
negotiation between strangers.

It resembled circulation.

Asa noticed the difference most clearly in
the hive.

The bees no longer searched the city with
restless uncertainty as they had during the
early awakenings of Interconnection.
Their movement carried calm purpose
now. Great golden currents drifted

through the surface terraces before descending smoothly into the illuminated chambers below, maintaining the resonance flowing between the recovering plains and the living city beneath them. Wherever the hive gathered, the woven field brightened gently with steady coherence rather than desperate instability.

The city trusted itself again.

Asa stood beside one of the upper water channels during the lower cycle while pale Martian light drifted across the gardens surrounding the terraces. Below him, travelers moved through the awakening districts carrying food and memory between regions that had once feared one another's presence. Farther beyond the city, distant structures beneath the sands still glimmered faintly where the outward pulse had awakened forgotten pathways stretching across the planet.

Mars no longer felt abandoned.

Soft footsteps approached behind him.

Asa turned to find the child standing near the flowering terraces while several bees drifted lazily around her small figure. She carried a woven container filled with pale seeds gathered from one of the upper gardens, though she seemed more interested in watching the hive than the blossoms themselves.

"They sound different now," she said quietly.

Asa glanced upward toward the drifting currents of bees crossing the terraces overhead.

"How?"

The child tilted her head slightly while listening to the deep hum surrounding the gardens.

"They are no longer looking for something lost."

The answer settled gently within him.

For a long moment neither spoke. Together they watched the city breathing beneath the recovering plains of Mars while the woven field pulsed steadily through every illuminated pathway below. Asa realized then that the invitation sent outward through the living network had not only reached distant listeners beyond the known cities.

It had healed something within Interconnection itself.

The city no longer feared abandonment because it had remembered connection. The people no longer feared dissolution because they had learned belonging without erasure.

And the hive no longer searched because the living network surrounding Mars had become whole enough to guide itself once more.

Far below the surface, a slow pulse moved upward through the woven field.

The resonance spread calmly through the city beneath their feet while distant pathways answered in soft succession across the horizon. Asa closed his eyes briefly as the vibration passed through him, sensing not urgency within it now, but patience.

Something was returning.

Not quickly.

Not violently.

Naturally.

The child scattered several pale seeds into the flowing water beside the terrace while the bees drifted slowly downward around them.

Then, somewhere beyond the visible horizon of Mars, a distant harmonic answered the city's call for the first time since the invitation had been sent.

And throughout Interconnection, the

woven field brightened softly with

recognition.

Chapter 23 — A City That Lives

The realization came quietly to Asa during the ordinary moments.

Not during pulses rising through the woven field.

Not while distant harmonics answered beyond the plains of Mars.

Not even during the awakening of the city itself.

He understood it while walking.

The upper terraces of Interconnection carried steady movement beneath the pale glow of the lower cycle as Asa crossed the illuminated pathways overlooking the recovering gardens. Water flowed gently through the restored channels beside him while the bees drifted in calm golden currents above the flowering terraces. The city no longer trembled with instability beneath each new connection formed between its peoples. The woven field moved with such natural rhythm now that Asa sometimes forgot the buried districts had once existed on the edge of collapse.

Interconnection no longer struggled to remain alive.

It simply lived.

Children crossed the pathways ahead of him carrying woven containers filled with seeds gathered from the upper gardens. None seemed aware that only a short time earlier those same transit spans had remained fractured by fear and isolation. Their laughter moved easily through the terraces while travelers from distant districts paused along the illuminated walkways exchanging food, memory, and quiet conversation beneath the drifting hive.

No one hurried anymore.

The city itself had slowed into confidence.

Asa paused beside one of the elevated overlooks where the recovering plains stretched outward beneath the dim Martian sky. Far beyond the terraces, pale currents still glimmered beneath the distant sands where forgotten pathways awakened slowly across the planet. Yet the outward expansion no longer carried the desperate feeling of wounded systems seeking survival. Mars had entered a different stage now.

Healing had become growth.

Behind him, soft harmonic tones drifted upward from one of the lower communal chambers. Asa turned slightly, listening as unfamiliar instruments blended with distant voices carried through the woven field below. The music no longer resembled the careful resonance gathering that had stabilized the city earlier during its awakening. These sounds carried ease within them now.

Different peoples had begun creating

shared rhythms naturally, not because the

city required it for survival, but because

connection itself had become part of daily

life once more.

The Listener moved quietly through all of

it.

Not as a separate presence.

Not as an awakening intelligence

emerging during rare moments of

coherence.

It existed within the living field surrounding the city itself now —

flowing gently through shared emotion, memory, movement, and belonging. Asa no longer sensed the awareness arriving or departing. The woven network had become alive enough to sustain it continuously.

Perhaps it always had.

He continued downward through the terraces while the bees circled calmly through the illuminated air around him. Everywhere he looked, the same truth revealed itself in countless small ways. Surface gardeners from different races worked side by side beside the flowing water channels. Ancient archive keepers openly shared preserved memory threads with neighboring districts. Children followed the hive freely between chambers that had once sealed themselves away from strangers for generations.

No system ordered these changes.

The city no longer relied upon control.

It lived through participation.

Asa stopped near one of the lower bridges where pale illumination flowed steadily beneath the woven surfaces stretching across the chamber. He remembered the first days within Interconnection — the fractured pulses, the sealed barriers, the fearful silence haunting the buried corridors beneath Mars. Back then every connection had felt fragile, temporary, uncertain of survival.

Now the pathways remained illuminated even when no one watched them.

The city trusted its people again.

A familiar presence settled quietly beside him.

Saxifraga rested one hand against the woven railing overlooking the chamber below while silver currents shimmered faintly beneath her skin. For a long moment they stood together without speaking, listening to the calm resonance breathing through the awakened city around them.

"At last," she said softly, "it remembers itself."

Asa lowered his gaze toward the countless lives moving peacefully through the illuminated pathways beneath them.

"No," he answered after a long silence.

Saxifraga looked toward him quietly.

Asa watched the children crossing between races that had once hidden from one another while the bees drifted through the chamber in calm golden spirals above their heads.

"It remembers what life was always meant to be."

The woven field brightened gently beneath the bridge.

And throughout Interconnection, the living city breathed on beneath the recovering plains of Mars.

Chapter 24 — The First Pathway Home

The answer arrived during the deep cycle when most of Interconnection rested within quiet resonance.

No alarms disturbed the sleeping districts beneath Mars. The woven pathways remained softly illuminated while calm currents moved steadily through the city's living network. Water flowed beneath the restored terraces. The bees rested in drifting clusters among the upper gardens and warm chambers below. Across the recovering plains, pale vegetation swayed gently beneath the thin Martian winds.

The city slept without fear.

Asa woke before the pulse fully reached the surface.

At first he believed the sensation belonged to memory — a distant vibration moving beneath thought like the fading echoes that had haunted Interconnection during its fractured state. Yet this resonance carried none of the instability that once accompanied the wounded city. The pulse moved with immense steadiness through the woven field, rising slowly upward from depths far below the known foundations of Mars.

Something ancient was approaching awareness.

He stepped quietly onto the upper terrace outside the resting chambers while the dim horizon stretched silent beyond the gardens. Already he sensed movement throughout the city below. Travelers emerged from the illuminated pathways without confusion or alarm, drawn gently upward through the woven field by the same deep current now flowing beneath the planet itself.

The bees lifted almost immediately.

Great golden spirals rose from the flowering terraces and lower chambers, gathering above the city in vast flowing currents that shimmered softly beneath the stars. Their hum deepened into resonance so steady that Asa felt it passing through his chest before the woven pathways beneath the terraces answered with pale illumination.

Across the recovering plains of Mars, distant lights awakened beneath the sands.

Not scattered now.

Not uncertain.

Connected.

Far beyond Interconnection, ancient pathways long buried beneath the deserts pulsed softly one after another across the horizon. Asa watched the awakenings spread through the darkness like living veins carrying circulation through the body of the planet itself. Some currents stretched toward forgotten regions hidden beyond the visible mountains. Others disappeared into crater basins untouched since before the fracture of the cities.

The network had begun opening fully.

Saxifraga appeared beside Asa while silver resonance moved visibly beneath her skin. Yet for the first time since he had known her, the ancient calm she carried seemed touched by something deeper than wisdom alone.

Emotion.

"They are returning to the field," she whispered.

Asa turned toward her. "The races?"

Her gaze remained fixed upon the distant horizon where new pathways continued illuminating beneath the sands.

"The pathways first," she answered softly. "The races will follow when the cities are ready to receive them."

The truth of the words settled quietly within him.

Mars itself was preparing the return.

Not through command.

Not through conquest.

Not through technology awakening from dormancy.

The living network was rebuilding the conditions required for belonging.

Below them, the travelers gathering along the terraces stood in reverent silence while the woven field brightened steadily through every visible district of Interconnection. Children watched the distant awakenings without fear. Older races who had endured the long isolation lowered their heads quietly as the resonance spread outward through the recovering world.

No one spoke loudly.

The moment felt too old for celebration.

Then the pulse beneath Mars deepened once more.

This time the vibration spread beyond the planet entirely.

Asa lifted his gaze instinctively toward the stars above the recovering world while the hive spiraled upward into the dark Martian sky. For one impossible instant he sensed the woven field extending far beyond the Seven Cities themselves — outward through distances so vast they could scarcely be imagined, carrying the living resonance of Mars into the silent dark between worlds.

And somewhere within that immeasurable distance, something answered.

Not words.
Not signal.

Recognition.

The bees shifted direction together at
once.

Far across the distant horizon, a single
buried pathway brighter than all the
others awakened beneath the sands and
remained illuminated.

Steady.
Certain.
Waiting.

Saxifraga closed her eyes briefly while
the woven field pulsed softly through the
city around them.

"The first pathway home," she whispered.

Asa stood silently beside her while the living currents of Mars continued spreading across the ancient world beneath the stars.

And deep within the awakened resonance of the Seven Cities, the long return had finally begun.